MAVIS

Based on *The Railway Series* by th ... Awdry

Illustrations by
Robin Davies and Creative Design

EGMONT

First published in Great Britain 2003
by Egmont Books Limited
239 Kensington High Street, London W8 6SA
All Rights Reserved

Thomas the Tank Engine & Friends

A BRITT ALLCROFT COMPANY PRODUCTION

Based on The Railway Series by The Rev W Awdry

© Gullane (Thomas) LLC 2003

ISBN 1 4052 0701 9
9 10 8
Printed in Great Britain

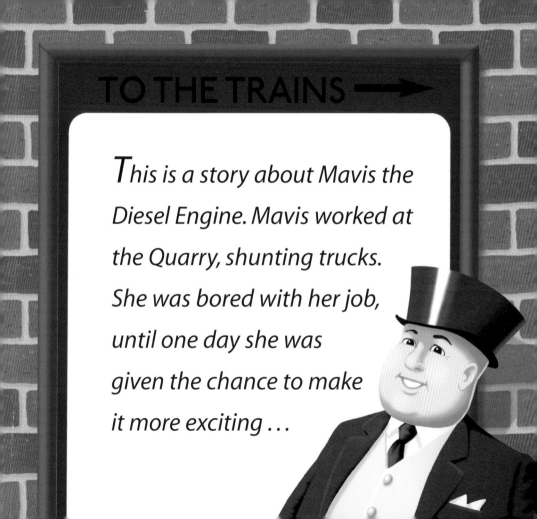

This is a story about Mavis the Diesel Engine. Mavis worked at the Quarry, shunting trucks. She was bored with her job, until one day she was given the chance to make it more exciting …

Mavis was a diesel engine who worked at the Quarry. She shunted trucks for other engines to collect.

Mavis was a young engine, and she liked to get her own way. She thought she knew better than everyone else.

Every day, Mavis would put Toby's trucks in a different place, so he had to search for them.

"Trucks should be where I can find them," said Toby, crossly.

"Nonsense!" said Mavis.

"I can't waste time arguing!" said Toby. "If you know so much, then take the trucks yourself!"

Mavis was very pleased. Taking trucks on Toby's branch line made her feel important.

So the next day, Mavis set off along the branch line with Toby's trucks. But the trucks didn't like bossy Mavis.

"It's frosty today. Let's play a trick on her!" they whispered.

Mavis travelled happily along Toby's line. Ahead of her was a level crossing, so she stopped carefully. "I'm so good at this. I don't need silly old Toby!" she laughed.

But she didn't know what the trucks were planning.

When it was time to move again, the trucks whispered to each other, "Hold back! Hold back!"

Mavis tried to set off, but her wheels just spun. She couldn't get a grip on the frosty ground. The Troublesome Trucks giggled and giggled.

The drivers of the cars and lorries waiting at the level crossing were getting very angry. But there was nothing Mavis could do!

Then Mavis saw Toby approaching in the distance. He had come to help.

"Having trouble, Mavis?" he smiled.

Mavis felt cross and silly. She had boasted to Toby that she knew best, and now she was stuck and Toby had to rescue her!

Toby was coupled to Mavis. He puffed and slipped, and at last he got Mavis and the trucks moving. Mavis hardly helped at all. She didn't even say 'thank you'.

When Mavis got back to the Quarry,
The Fat Controller was very cross with her.

"You are a naughty engine," he said.
"You will stay here in future!"

Mavis felt angry. She thought the Quarry
was boring. She wished she could go on
Toby's branch line again.

Soon spring arrived on Sodor. It was a very busy time at the Quarry. Every day, Mavis got the trucks ready for Toby. But she was never allowed to take them along Toby's branch line.

Then one day, Mavis had an idea. She said to the Troublesome Trucks: "When we get to the beginning of Toby's line, please will you bump me? Then I'll be on his line whether he likes it or not!"

"Yes! Yes! Yes!" giggled the trucks.

"I'll show that fusspot Toby," said Mavis to herself.

But when the time came, Mavis was busy elsewhere, so Toby shunted the trucks himself.

"Never mind," the trucks whispered to each other. "Let's bump Toby instead!"

So they gave Toby a big bump! He rushed on to his branch line much too fast. His Driver and Fireman were knocked over. Toby was out of control!

Toby couldn't stop! He rushed over the level crossing. Luckily there weren't any cars there.

Up ahead there was an old bridge. The river had flooded and part of the bridge had been washed away.

If Toby didn't stop before he reached it, he might fall in the river!

As Toby approached the bridge, the rails stretched across the gap, just like a tightrope!

His Driver braked hard but Toby slid along the track. His brakes squealed. He used every bit of his strength and stopped … just in time!

Mavis felt terrible. It was all her fault! So she rushed to the rescue. First she pulled the trucks back up the track. Then she helped pull Toby carefully away from the bridge.

"I'm sorry, Toby!" she said. "It's all my fault!"

"Never mind, Mavis," said Toby, kindly. "Thank you for rescuing me!"

After that day, Mavis and Toby became good friends. Mavis still bossed the trucks around at the Quarry, but she always listened to Toby's advice.

And sometimes, for a special treat, Toby would let Mavis take the trucks carefully along his branch line!

The Thomas Story Library is THE definitive collection of stories about Thomas and ALL his Friends.

5 more Thomas Story Library titles will be chuffing into your local bookshop in April 2006:

´Arry and Bert
George
Jack
Annie and Clarabel
Rheneas

And there are even more
Thomas Story Library books to follow later!
So go on, start your Thomas Story Library NOW!

A Fantastic Offer for Thomas the Tank Engine Fans!

In every Thomas Story Library book like this one, you will find a special token. Collect 6 Thomas tokens and we will send you a brilliant Thomas poster, and a double-sided bedroom door hanger!

Simply tape a £1 coin in the space above, and fill out the form overleaf.

Cut along the dotted line

TO BE COMPLETED BY AN ADULT

To apply for this great offer, ask an adult to complete the coupon below and send it with a pound coin and 6 tokens, to:
THOMAS OFFERS, PO BOX 715, HORSHAM RH12 5WG

☐ Please send a Thomas poster and door hanger. I enclose 6 tokens plus a £1 coin. (Price includes P&P)

Fan's name...

Address..

....Postcode..................................

Date of birth..

Name of parent/guardian..

Signature of parent/guardian..

Please allow 28 days for delivery. Offer is only available while stocks last. We reserve the right to change the terms of this offer at any time and we offer a 14 day money back guarantee. This does not affect your statutory rights.

☐ Data Protection Act: If you do not wish to receive other similar offers from us or companies we recommend, please tick this box. Offers apply to UK only.